The author has studied with the Academy of Children's Writers and has had
a couple of pieces of poetry published in the past. This is his debut children's book.

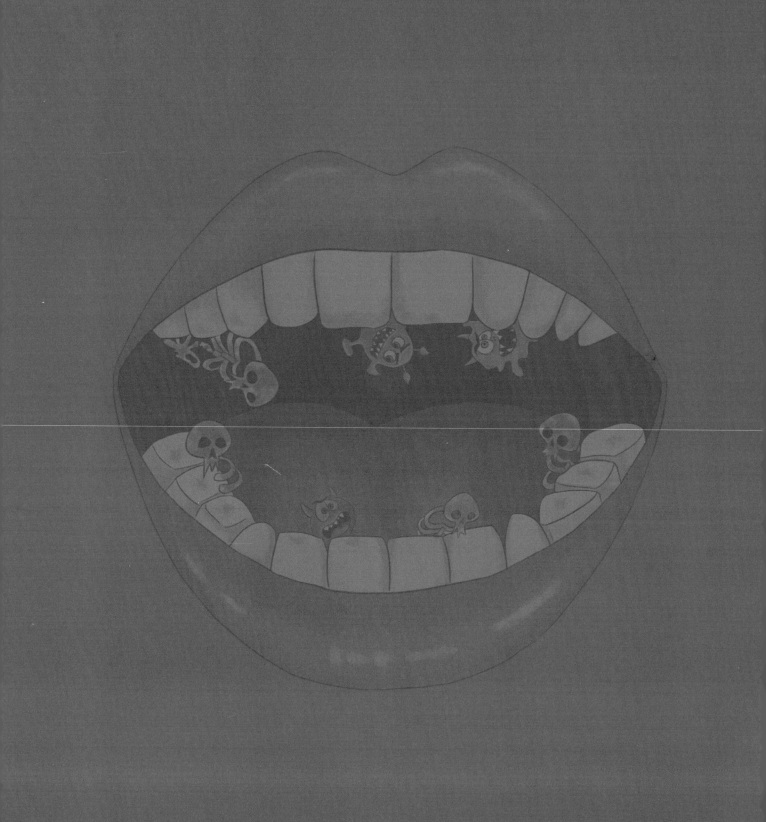

The Toothy Tale

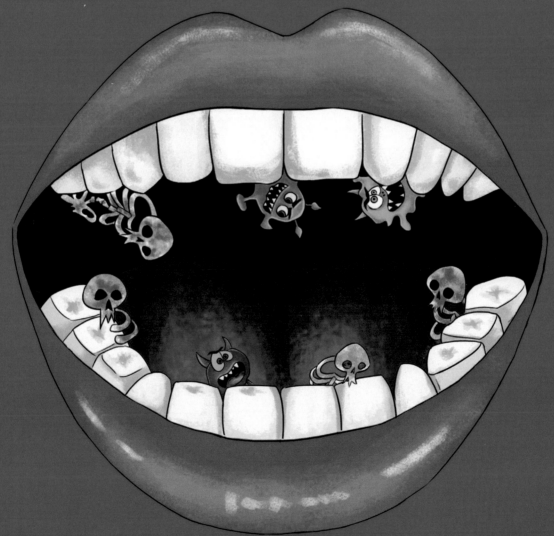

Michael Everest

AUSTIN MACAULEY PUBLISHERS™
LONDON · CAMBRIDGE · NEW YORK · SHARJAH

A CIP catalogue record for this title is available from the British Library.

ISBN 9781528930451 (Paperback)
ISBN 9781528966320 (ePub e-book)

www.austinmacauley.com

First Published (2021)
Austin Macauley Publishers Ltd
25 Canada Square
Canary Wharf
London
E14 5LQ

Jack sat in the dentist's chair. His mum held his hand.
"We should go, Mum, I should be practising my flute
for the school band."
She smiled, "You can practise tomorrow, dear."
Jack needed a filling and was full of fear.
I could escape, he thought, too late!

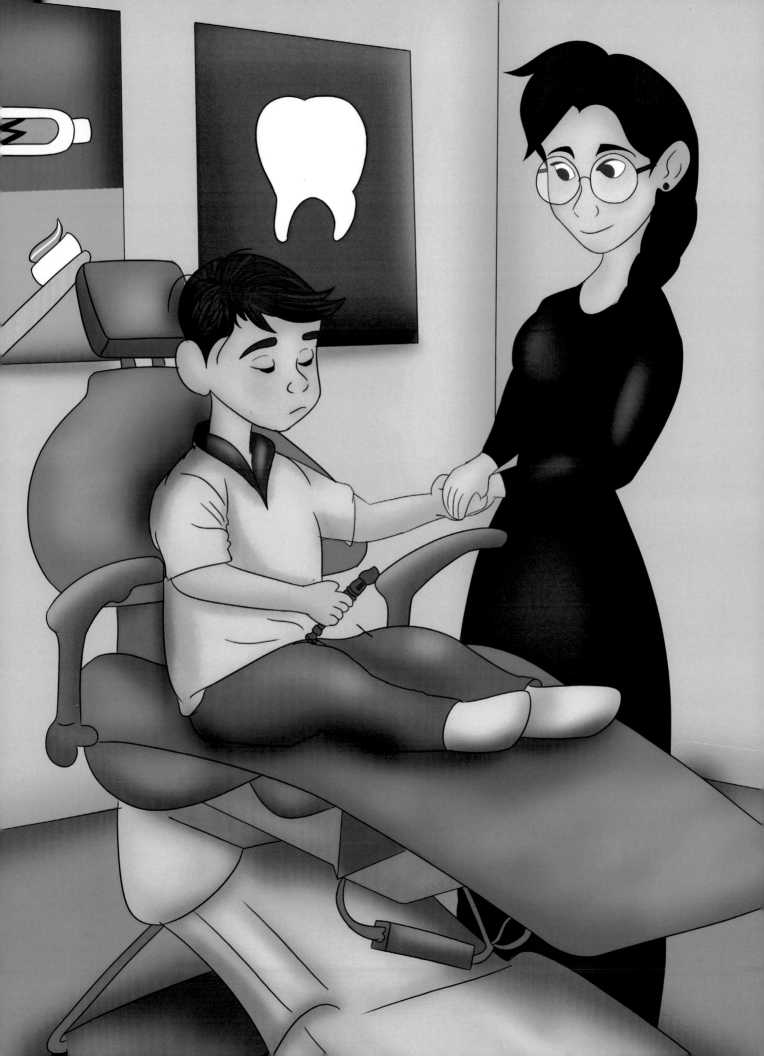

The dentist entered with a drill on a silver plate.
"Good morning," she boomed as she put on her gloves.

Jack looked at the ceiling above.
He heard the dreaded words, "Open wide."
The dentist peered inside.
"I'll give you an injection to numb the gum."

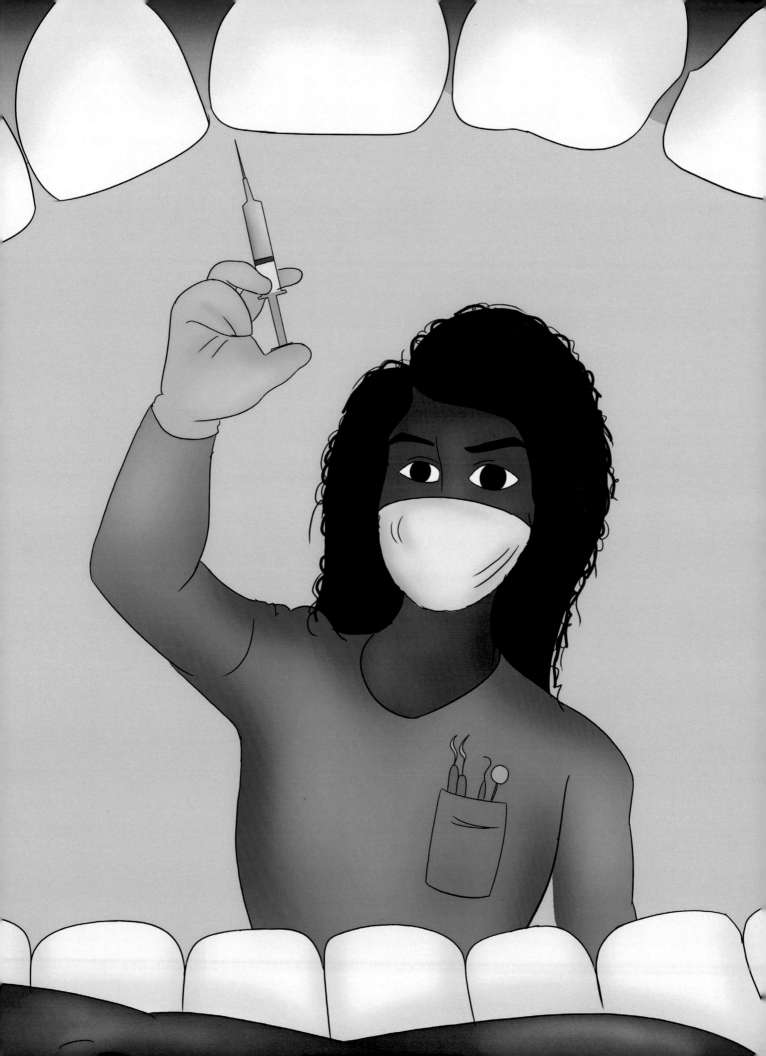

Jack gulped and stared at his mum.
"Ouch!" he cried as he felt the injection's sharpness.
He felt dizzy. Everything went into darkness.
"Get her!" The shout woke Jack. He jumped to his feet.
Where was he? It was dark, warm,
and he heard a drumbeat.
He couldn't believe it. He was standing on a tongue...
in a mouth!

"HELP, save me from the foul mouth!"
Jack ran towards the cry. He reached a line of teeth.

A girl in white was tied to a flagpole on a tooth. A bag was dropped on him with the words 'Save this from the thief'. WHOOSH! An arrow flew past his head. WHOOSH! Another made him jump behind the tooth.
He began to climb to find the truth.
"Get me down," she shouted. He pushed the pole.
She crashed down. "Sorry," he said like a silly soul.
He helped her up. "Who are you?"
"I am Sam the tooth treasurer, the tooth fairy's sister. That bag is full of money to give to her tonight for the children... Ooh!"
She stretched out her arm.

Below were a group of yellow skeletons.
They looked like they meant harm.
"What are they?" Jack asked, trying to flee.
"Plaque skeletons," she said.
"Put on this silver breastplate
under your shirt. Please protect me."
The skeletons climbed with axes and evil grins.
Jack kicked the first in the face.
He kicked the second in the shins.

He grabbed an axe and Sam's hand.
They slid down the tooth to the ground.
She snatched the bag, she couldn't fly, her wings were aching. A bad-breath zombie appeared without a sound.
It began its attack.
Jack smacked it over the head with an ear-splitting crack.
A big, dark, red-eyed Cyclops figure appeared.
It was what Sam feared.
"I've found you!" The growling voice sounded very menacing.
"It's Colonel Cavity! He's been chasing me," she said, trembling.

"Give me the money to eat, or I'll eat you both," he said, drooling in the same horrible voice.
"It's your choice!"
Sam saw a gap in the teeth for her escape...
Jack would have to fight him.
"I must escape," she shouted. "Goodbye!"

Jack looked grim!
Suddenly, a large drill came down on the nearest tooth.
It began drilling
It was Jack's filling!
Jack awoke. His mum smiled.
"All over, Jack...but we can't go yet."
She frowned, "You look upset."

"Mum, Mum, I was in a mouth,
I had to save the tooth fairy's sister from Colonel
Cavity...it..."
The dentist smiled. "You were dreaming.
Now go and relax for a bit."
Jack walked into the empty waiting room.
There stood Colonel Cavity with the bag... his prize!
Jack had been in his own mouth after all.
What a surprise!
"I managed to escape by jumping on the drill."
Cavity growled, "I have the money, I have won,
now out of the way!"

Suddenly, Sam flew in, a laser bolt fired from her wand that hit Cavity and made him stumble and sway.
"Squirt him with the toothpaste," she cried.
Jack grabbed a tube and squirted; Cavity's face burnt like toxic waste.
"YEARGHH!!!!" he screamed. He ran to the window in haste!
Sam retrieved the bag. "I've no energy, you need to play a tune to help me fly!"
Jack gulped. He rolled up a leaflet on the table into a flute, he had to try.
He played his tune. Amazingly, out of the flute flew a blue troll!!!!
It charged at Cavity and pushed him through the open window!!!
Sam leapt on the troll, her wings flapping. "Thank you!"
She flew away...waving goodbye.
He too waved goodbye.
Jack's mum walked in. "If your tooth had been taken out, the Tooth Fairy could have visited and left you a few pence."
Jack smiled and tapped his breastplate, "Tooth Fairy? Sorry, Mum...but I don't believe in all that childish nonsense!"